# My Mother's Rival

Charlotte M. Brame

EVERYDAY LIFE LIBRARY No. 4

Published by EVERYDAY LIFE, Chicago

MY MOTHER'S RIVAL

By CHARLOTTE M. BRAEME

*Author of "Dora Thorne," "The Belle of Lynn," "The Mystery of Colde Fell," "Madolin's Lover," "Coralie," Etc., Etc.*

## CHAPTER I.

I have often wondered if the world ever thinks of what becomes of the children of great criminals who expiate their crime on the scaffold. Are they taken away and brought up somewhere in ignorance of who or what they are? Does some kind relative step forward always bring them up under another name?

There is great criminal trial, and we hear that the man condemned to death leaves two daughters and a son—what becomes of them can any one living say? Who meets them in after life? Has any young man ever been pointed out to you as the son of Mr. So-and-so, the murderer? Has any young woman been pointed out to you as his daughter?

It is not long since all England was interested in the trial of a so-called gentleman for murder. He was found guilty, condemned and executed. At the time of the trial all the papers spoke of his little son—a fair-haired little lad, who was as unconscious of all that happened as a little babe. I have often wondered what became of him. Does he hear his father's name? Do those with whom he lives know him for a murderer's son? If he goes wooing any fair-faced girl, will she be afraid of marrying him lest, in the coming years, she may suffer the same fate his mother did? Does that same son, when he reads of criminals and scaffolds, wince, and shudder, and grow sick at heart?

And the daughters, do they grow old and die before their time? Do they hide themselves under false names in silent places, dreading lest the world should know them? Does any man ever woo them? Are they ever happy wives and mothers?

I have thought much on this subject, because I, who write this story, seem to the world one of the most commonplace people in it, and yet I have lived, from the time I was a child, in the midst of a tragedy dark as any that ever saddened this fair land.

No one knows it, no one guesses it. People talk of troubles, of romances, of sad stories and painful histories before me, but no one ever guessed that I have known perhaps the saddest of all. My heart learned to ache as the first lesson it learned in life.

When I think of those unhappy children who go about the world with so dark a secret locked in their hearts, I think of myself, and what I hold locked in my heart.

Read for yourself, dear reader, and tell me if you think there have been many fates in this world harder than mine.

My Name is Laura Tayne, and my home Tayne Abbey, in the grand old County of Kent. The Taynes were of good family, not very ancient—the baronetcy is quite a modern one, dating from George the First—but Tayne Abbey is one of the grandest old buildings in England. Whenever I looked at it I thought of those beautiful, picturesque, haunted houses that one sees in Christmas annuals, with Christmas lights shining from the great windows. I am sorry to say that I know very little of architecture. I could not describe Tayne Abbey; it was a dark, picturesque, massive building; the tall towers were covered with ivy, the large windows were wreathed with flowers of every hue. In some parts of sweet, sunny Kent the flowers grow as though they were in a huge hothouse; they did so at Tayne Abbey, for the front stood to the west, and there were years when it seemed to be nothing but summer.

The great oriel windows—the deep bay windows, large as small rooms—the carved oaken panels, the finely painted ceilings, the broad corridors, the beautiful suites of rooms—all so bright, light and lofty—the old-fashioned porch and the entrance hall, the grand sweep of terraces one after another, the gardens, the grounds, the park, were all perfection in their way. To make the picture quite complete, close to us—joined, indeed, by a subterranean passage, for the existence of which no one could account—stood the ruins of what had once been the real Abbey of Tayne—a fine old abbey that, in the time of "bluff King Hal," had been inhabited by the monks of St. Benedict. They were driven away, and the abbey and lands were given to the family of De Montford. The De Montfords did not prosper; after some generations the abbey fell into ruins, and then they sold the abbey to the Taynes, who had long wished for it on account of the similarity of names. Our ancestors built the present mansion called Tayne Abbey; each succeeding Tayne had done something to beautify it—one had built the magnificent picture gallery, and had made a magnificent collection of pictures, so magnificent, indeed, as to rob the Taynes for many years afterward of some part of their revenue. There they stood still, a fortune in themselves. Another Tayne had devoted himself to collecting gold and silver plate; in no other house in England was there such a collection of valuable plate as in ours. A third Tayne had thought of nothing but his gardens, devoting his time, thoughts and money to them until they were wonderful to behold. There were no square and round beds of different flowers, arranged with mathematical precision; the white lilies stood in great white sheaves, the eucharis lilies grew tall and stately, the grand arum lily reared its deep chalice, the lovely lily of the valley shot its white bells; there were every variety of carnation, of sweet williams, of sweet peas, of the old-fashioned southernwood and pansy; there grew crocus, snowdrop and daffadowndilly; great lilac trees, and the white auricula were there in abundance; there, too, stood a sun-dial and a fine fountain. It was a garden to please a poet and a painter; but I have to tell the story of the lives of human beings, and not of flowers.

The first memory that comes to me is of my beautiful young mother; the mention of her name brings me the vision of a fair face with hair of bright gold, and deep, large, blue eyes; of soft silken dresses, from the folds of which came the sweetest perfume; of fine trailing laces, fine as the intricate work of a spider's web; of white hands, always warm and soft, and covered with sparkly rings; of a sweet, low voice, that was like the cooing of a dove. All these things come back to me as I write the word "mother." My father, Sir Roland Tayne, was a hearty, handsome, pleasure-loving man. No one ever saw him dull, or cross, or angry; he was liberal, generous, and beloved.

He worships my beautiful young mother, and he worshiped me. Every one said I was the very image of mama. I had the same golden hair and deep-blue eyes; the same shaped face and hands. I remember that my mother—that sweet young mother—never walked steadily when she was out with me. It was as though she could not help dancing like a child.

"Come along, baby darling," she would say to me, "let us get away from them all, and have a race."

She called me "baby" until I was nearly six—for no other came to take my place. I heard the servants speak of me, and say what a great heiress I would be in the years to come, if my father had no sons; but I hardly understood, and cared still less.

As I grew older I worshipped my beautiful mother, she was so very kind to me. I always felt that she was so pleased to see me. She never gave me the impression that I was tiresome, or intruded on her. Sometimes her toilet would be finished before the dinner-bell rang, then she would come to the nursery and ask for me. We walked up and down the long picture gallery, where the dead, and gone Ladies Tayne looked at us from the walls. No face there was so fair as my mother's. She was more beautiful than a picture, with her golden hair and fair face, her sweeping dresses and trailing laces.

The tears rise even now, hot and bitter, to my eyes when I think of those happy hours—my intense pride in and devoted love for my mother. How lightly I held her hand, how I kissed her lovely trailing laces.

"Mamma," I said to her, one day, "it is just like coming to heaven when you call me to walk with you."

"You will know a better heaven some day," she said, laughingly; "but I have not known it yet."

What was there she did not do? She sang until the music seemed to float round the room; she drew and painted, and she danced. I have seen no one like her. They said she was like an angel in the house; so young, so fair, so sweet—so young, yet, in her wise, sweet way, a mother and friend to the whole household. Even the maids, when they had done anything wrong and feared the housekeeper, would ask my mother to intercede for them.

If she saw a servant who had been crying, she did not rest until she knew the cause of the tears. If it were a sick mother, then money and wine would be dispatched. I have heard since that even if their love affairs went wrong, it was always "my lady" who set them right, and many a happy marriage took place from Tayne Abbey.

It was just the same with the poor on the estate; she was a friend to each one, man, woman or child. Her face was like a sunbeam in the

4

cottages, yet she was by no means unwise or indiscriminate in her charities. When the people had employment she gave nothing but kind words; where they were industrious, and could not get work, she helped them liberally; where they were idle, and would not work, "my lady" lectured with grave sweetness that was enough to convert the most hardened sinner.

Every one sought her in distress, her loving sweetness of disposition was so well known. Great ladies came from London sometimes, looking world-worn and weary, longing for comfort and sympathy. She gave it so sweetly, no wonder they had desired it.

It was the same thing on our own estate. If husband and wife quarreled, it was to my mother they appealed—if a child seemed inclined to go wrong, the mother at once came to her for advice.

Was it any wonder that I, her only child, loved her so passionately when every one else found her so sweet, beautiful and good?

## CHAPTER II.

Lady Conyngham, who was one of the most beautiful and fashionable women in London, came to spend a week with my mother. I knew from different little things that had been said she had some great trouble with her husband, but of course I did not know in the least what it was about.

As a rule, my mother sent me away on some pretext or other when they had their long conversations; on this particular day she forgot me. When Lady Conyngham began to talk I was behind my mother's chair with a book of fairy tales. The first thing that aroused my attention was a sob from Lady Conyngham and my mother saying to her:

"It is quite useless, you know, Isabel, to struggle against the inevitable."

"It is very well for you, Beatrice, to talk in that fashion, you who have never had a trouble in your own life; now, have you?"

"No," replied my beautiful mother, "not a real trouble, thank Heaven," and she clasped her white hands in gratitude.

"Then you cannot judge. You mean well, I know, when you advise me to be patient; but, Beatrice, suppose it were your husband, what should you do?"

"I should do just what I am advising you to do; I should be patient, Isabel."

"You would. If Sir Roland neglected you, slighted you, treated you with indifference, harder to bear than hate, if he persisted in thrusting the presence of your rivals on you, what should you do?"

"Do you mean to ask me, really and truly, what I should do in that case?" asked my dear mother. "Oh, Isabel, I can soon tell you that; I should die."

"Die—nonsense!" cried Lady Conyngham. "What is the use of dying?—the very thing they want. I will not die;" but my mother had laid her fair head back on the velvet pillow, and her eyes lingered on the clear blue sky. Was she looking for the angels who must have heard her voice?

"I am not as strong as you, Isabel," she said, gently, "and I love Sir Roland with my whole heart."

"I loved my husband with my whole heart," sobbed the beautiful woman, "and I have done nothing in this world to deserve what I have suffered. I loved him with a pure, great affection—what became of it? Three days after we were married I saw him myself patting one of the maids—a good-looking one, you may be sure—on the cheek."

"Perhaps he meant no harm," said my mother, consolingly; "you know that gentlemen do not attach so much importance as we do to these little trifles."

"You try, Beatrice, how you would like it; you have been married ten years, and even at this date you would not like Sir Roland to do such a thing?"

"I am sure I should not; but then, you know, there are men and men. Sir Roland is graver in character than Lord Conyngham. What would mean much from one, means little from the other."

So, with sweet, wise words, she strove to console and comfort this poor lady, who had evidently been stricken to the heart in some way or another. I often thought of my mother's words, "I should die," long after Lady Conyngham had made some kind of reconciliation with her husband, and had gone back to him. I thought of my mother's face, as she leaned back to watch the sky, crying out, "I should die."

I knew that I ought not to have sat still; my conscience reproached me very much; but when I did get up to go away mamma did not notice me. From that time it was wonderful how much I thought of "husbands." They were to me the most mysterious people in the world—a race quite apart from other men. When they spoke of any one as being Mrs. or Lady S——'s husband, to me he became a wicked man at once. Some were good; some bad. Some seemed to trust their wives; others to be rather frightened than otherwise at them. I studied intently all the different varieties of husbands. I heard my father laugh often, and say:

"Bless the child, how intently she looks and listens."

He little knew that I was trying to find out for myself, and by my mother's wit, which were good husbands and which were bad. I did not like to address any questions to my parents on the subject, lest they should wonder why the subject interested me.

Once, when I was with my mother—we were walking up and down the picture gallery—I did venture to ask her:

"Mamma, what makes husbands bad? Why do they make their wives cry?"

How my beautiful mother looked at me. There were laughter, fun and pain in her eyes altogether.

"What makes my darling ask such a question?" she replied. "I am very surprised: it is such a strange question for my Laura to ask! I hope all husbands are good."

"No, not all," I hastened to answer; "Lady Conyngham's was not—I heard her say so."

"I am sorry you heard it—you must not repeat it; you are much too young to talk about husbands, Laura."

Of course I did not mention then again—equally of course I did not think less of this mysterious kind of beings.

My beautiful mother was very happy with her husband, Sir Roland—she loved him exceedingly, and he was devoted to her. The other ladies said he spoiled her, he was so attentive, so devoted, so kind. I have met with every variety of species which puzzled my childish mind, but none so perfect as he was then.

"You do not know what trouble means, dear Lady Tayne." "With a husband like yours, life is all sunshine." "You have been spoiled with kindness!"

All these exclamations I used to hear, until I became quite sure that my father was the best husband in the world.

On my tenth birthday my father would have a large ball, and he insisted that I should be present at it. My mother half hesitated, but he insisted; so, thanks to him, I have one perfectly happy memory. I thought far more of my beautiful mother than myself. I stood in the hall, watching her as she came down the great staircase, great waves of shining silk and trailing laces making her train, diamonds gleaming in her golden hair, her white neck and arms bare; so tall, slender and stately, like the picture of some lovely young queen. Papa and I stood together watching her.

"Let me kiss her first!" I cried, running to her.

"Mind the lace and diamonds, Laura," he cried.

"Never mind either, my darling," she said laughingly. "One kiss from you is worth more than all."

Sir Roland kissed her and stood looking at her with admiring eyes.

"Do you know, Beatrice," he said, "that you grow younger and more beautiful? It is dead swindle! I shall be a gray-bearded old man by the time you have grown quite young again."

My sweet mother! she evidently enjoyed his praise; she touched his face with her pretty hand.

"Old or young, Roland," she said, lovingly, "my heart will never change in its great love for you."

They did not know how intensely I appreciated this little scene.

"Here is a good husband," I said to myself, like the impertinent little critic I was; "this is not like Lady Conyngham's husband!" — the truth being that I could never get that unfortunate man quite out of my mind.

That night, certainly the very happiest of my life, my father danced with me. Heaven help me! I can remember my pride as I stood by the tall, stalwart figure, just able with the tips of my fingers to touch his arm. Mamma danced with me, too, and my happiness was complete. I watched all the ladies there, young and old; there was not one so fair as my mother. Closing my eyes, so tired of this world's sunlight, I see her again as I saw her that night, queen of the brilliant throng, the fairest woman present. I see her with her loving heart full of emotion kissing my father. I see her in the ballroom, the most graceful figure present.

I remember how every half-hour she came to speak to me and see if I were happy, and once, when she thought I was warm and tired, she took my hand and led me into the beautiful cool conservatory, where we sat and talked until I had grown cool again. I see her talking with queenly grace and laughing eyes, no one forgotten or neglected, partners found for the least attractive girls, while the sunshine of her presence was everywhere. She led a cotillion. I remember seeing her stand waiting the signal, the very type of grace and beauty.

Oh, my darling, if I were with you! As I saw her then I never saw her more.

I was present the next morning when my father and mother discussed the ball.

"How well you looked, Beatrice," said my father.

"How well I felt," she replied. "I am quite sure, Roland, that I enjoy dancing far better now than I did before I was married. I should like dancing parties a little oftener; they are much more amusing than your solemn dinner parties."

But, ah me! the dancing feet were soon to be stilled; all the rest of that summer there was something mysterious—every one was so solicitous about my mother—they seemed to think of nothing but her health. She was gay and charming herself, laughing at the fuss, anxiety and care. Sir Roland was devoted to her; he never left her. She took no more rides now on her favorite Sir Tristam, my father drove her carefully in the carriage; there were no more balls or parties; "extreme quiet and repose" seemed to be the keynote. Mamma was always "resting."

"She cannot want rest," I exclaimed, "when she does nothing to tire her! Oh, let me go to her!" for some foolish person had started a theory that I tired her. I who worshiped her, who would have kept silence for a year rather than have disturbed her for one moment! I appealed to Sir Roland, and he consulted her; the result was that I was permitted to steal into her boudoir, and, to my childish mind, it seemed that during those days my mother's heart and mine grew together.

## CHAPTER III.

It was a quiet Christmas at Tayne Abbey; we had no visitors, for my mother required the greatest care; but she did not forget one person in the house, or one on the estate. Sir Roland laughed when he saw the preparations—the beef, the blankets, the clothing of all kinds, the innumerable presents, for she had remembered every one's wants and needs. Sir Roland laughed.

"My dearest Beatrice," he said; "this will cost far more than a houseful of guests."

"Never mind the cost," she said; "it will bring down a blessing on us."

A quiet, beautiful Christmas. My father was in the highest of spirits, and would have the house decorated with holly and mistletoe. He went out to a few parties, but he was always unwilling to leave my mother, though she wished him to go; then, when we were quite alone, the wind wailing, the snow falling and beating up against the windows, she would ask me to read to her the beautiful gospel story of the star in the East and the child born in the stable because there was no room for Him in the inn. I read it to her over and over again; then we used to talk about it. She loved to picture the streets of Bethlehem, the star in the East, the herald angels, the shepherds who came from over the hills.

She was never tired, and I wondered why that story, more than any other, interested her so greatly.

I knew afterward.

It was February; the snowdrops were peeping above the ground; the yellow and purple crocuses appeared; in the clear, cold air there was a faint perfume of violets, and the terrible sorrow of our lives began.

I had gone to bed very happy one night, for my fair young mother had been most loving to me. She had been lying on the sofa in her boudoir all day; her luncheon and dinner had been carried to her, and, as a great privilege, I had been permitted to share them with her. She looked very pale and beautiful, and she was most loving to me. When I bade her good-night she held me in her arms as though

12

she would never let me go. What words she whispered to me—so loving that I have never forgotten them, and never shall while my memory lives. Twice she called me back when I had reached the door to say good-night again—twice I went back and kissed the pale, sweet face. It was very pale the last time, and I was frightened.

"Mamma, darling," I asked, "are you very ill?"

"Why, Laura?" she questioned.

"Because you look so pale, and you are always lying here. You never move about or dance and play as you used to do."

"But I will, Laura. You will see, the very first game we play at hare and hounds I shall beat you. God bless my darling child!"

That night seemed to me very strange. There was no rest and no silence. What could every one be doing? I heard the opening and closing of the doors, the sound of many footsteps in the dead of the night. I heard the galloping of horses and a carriage stop at the hall door. I thank Heaven even now that I did not connect these things with the illness of my mother. Such a strange night! and when morning light came there was no nurse to dress me. I lay wondering until, at last, Emma came, her face pale, her eyes swollen with tears.

"What has been the matter?" I cried. "Oh, Emma, what a strange night it has been! I have heard all kinds of noises. Has anything been wrong?"

"No, my dear," she replied.

But I felt quite sure she was keeping something from me.

"Emma, you should not tell stories!" I cried, so vehemently that she was startled. "You know how Heaven punished Ananias and Saphira for their wickedness."

"Hush, missie!" said my good nurse; "I have told no stories—I speak the truth; there is nothing wrong. See, I want you to have your breakfast here in your room this morning, and then Sir Roland wants you."

"How is mamma?" I asked.

"You shall go to her afterward," was the evasive reply.

"But how is she?" I persisted. "You do not say how she is."

"I am not my lady's maid, missie," she replied.

And then my heart sank. She would not tell a story, and she could not say my mother was better.

My breakfast was brought, but I could not eat it; my heart was heavy, and then Emma said it was time I went to papa.

When the door of my room was opened the silence that reigned over the house struck me with a deadly chill. What was it? There was no sound—no bells ringing, no footsteps, no cheery voices; even the birds that mamma loved were all quiet—the very silence and quiet of death seemed to hang over the place. I could feel the blood grow cold in my veins, my heart grow heavy as lead, my face grew pale as death, but I would say no more of my fears to Emma.

She opened the library door, where she said Sir Roland was waiting for me, and left me there.

I went in and sprang to my father's arms—my own clasped together round his neck—looking eagerly in his face.

Ah, me! how changed it was from the handsome, laughing face of yesterday—so haggard, so worn, so white, and I could see that he had shed many tears.

"My little Laura—my darling," he said, "I have something to tell you—something which has happened since you bade dear mamma good-night."

"Oh, not to her!" I cried, in an agony of tears; "not to her!"

"Mamma is living," he said, and I broke from his arms. I flung myself in an agony of grief on the ground. Those words, "Mamma is living," seemed to me only little less terrible than those I had dreaded to hear—

"Mamma is dead."

Ah, my darling, it would have been better had you died then.

"Laura," said my father, gravely, "you must try and control yourself. You are only a child, I know, but it is just possible"—and here his

14

voice quivered—"it is just possible that you might be useful to your mother."

That was enough. I stood erect to show him how brave I could be.

Then he took me in his arms.

"My dearest little Laura," he said, "two angels have been with us during the night—the angel of life and the angel of death. You have had a little brother, but he only lived one hour. Now he is dead, and mamma is very dangerously ill. Tho doctors say that unless she has most perfect rest she will not get better—there must not be a sound in the house."

A little brother! At first my child's mind was so filled with wonder I could not realize what it meant. How often I had longed for brothers and sisters! Now I had had one, and he was dead before I could see him.

"I should like to see my little brother, papa—if I may," I said.

He paused thoughtfully for a few minutes, then answered:

"I am quite sure you may, Laura; I will take you."

We went, without making even the faintest sound, to the pretty rooms that had been set aside as nurseries. One of them had been beautifully decorated with white lace and flowers. There in the midst stood the berceaunette in which I had lain when I was a child.

My father took me up to it—at first I saw only the flowers, pale snowdrops and blue violets with green leaves; then I saw a sweet waxen face with closed eyes and lips.

Oh! baby brother, how often I have longed to be at rest with you! I was not frightened; the beautiful, tiny face, now still in death, had no horrors for me.

"May I kiss him, papa?" I asked. Oh, baby brother, why not have stayed with us for a few hours at least? I should like to have seen his pretty eyes and to have seen him just once with him lips parted; as it was, they were closed in the sweet, silent smile of death.

"Papa, what name should you have given him had he lived?" I asked.

"Your mother's favorite name—Gerald," he replied. "Ah, Laura, had he lived, poor little fellow, he would have been 'Sir Gerald Tayne, of Tayne Abbey.' How much dies in a child—who knows what manner of man this child might have been or what he might have done?"

"Papa, what is the use of such a tiny life?" I asked.

"Not even a philosopher could answer that question," said my father.

I kissed the sweet, baby face again and again. "Good-by, my little brother," I said. Ah! where shall I see his face again?

## CHAPTER IV.

My mother was in danger and my baby brother dead. The gloom that lay over our house was something never to be forgotten; the silence that was never broken by one laugh or one cheerful word, the scared faces—for every one loved "my lady." One fine morning, when the snowdrops had grown more plentiful, and there was a faint sign of the coming spring in the air, they took my baby brother to bury him. Such a tiny coffin, such tiny white wreaths, a little white pall covered with flowers. My father would not let black come near him.

My father wept bitter tears.

"There sleeps my little son and heir, Laura," he said to me—"my little boy. It is as though he had just peeped out of Heaven at this world, and, not liking it, had gone back again."

A pretty little white monument was put up to the baby Gerald. My mother chose the epitaph, which I had always thought so pretty. It was simply this—"The angels gather such lilies for God."

By degrees some little sunshine stole back, the dreadful silence lessened, the servants began to walk about without list slippers, the birds were carried back to the beautiful aviary—my mother's favorite nook; the doctors smiled as they came down the grand staircase. I heard Sir Roland whistling and singing as he had done weeks ago.

At last I was admitted to see her. One fine March morning, when the wind was blowing freshly and tossing the big, bare branches, I was taken to her room. I should not have known her; a pale, languid lady lay there in the place of my laughing, beautiful mother; two large blue eyes full of tears looked at me; two thin, white arms clasped me, and then I was lying on my mother's heart. Oh, my darling, if we could have died then.

"My little Laura, I was afraid I should never see you again," whispered a faint voice.

Ah, me, the ecstasy of the next half-hour! I sat close by her side and told her how the snowdrops were growing and the purple and golden crocuses made the garden seem quite gay. I told her where I had found the first violets, some of which I had brought to her. I cannot tell what it was like to me to feel my mother's hand on my head once more.

Then came a brief time of happiness. My mother improved a little, and was carried from the bedroom where she had spent so many weeks to her boudoir, and I was allowed to be with her all day.

"She would be better soon and able to go out," my father said, and then the happy old times would come back again. My mother would walk with me through the picture gallery at sunset, and more, she would dance with flying feet and run races with me in the wood. Oh, how I longed for the time when she would regain the color in her face and light in her eyes! They said I must be patient, it would come in time. But, alas! it was weary waiting; the days seemed as weeks to me, and yet my dear, beautiful mother was still confined to her room and to her bed. So it went on.

The ash buds grew black in March, the pine thorns fell in April, and yet she was still lying helpless on the sofa.

One day papa and I were both sitting with her. She looked better, and was talking to us about the nightingales she had heard last May in the woods.

"I feel better this morning," she said. "I am quite sure, Roland, that I could walk now if those tiresome doctors would let me."

"It is better to be careful, my darling," said papa; "they must know best."

"I am sure I could walk," said my mother, "and I feel such a restless longing to put my foot to the ground once more."

There was a bright flush on her face, and suddenly, without another word, she rose from her recumbent position on the sofa and stood quite upright. My father sprang from his chair with a little anxious cry. She tried to take one step forward, and fell with her face on the ground.

Ah, me! it was the old story over again, of silent gloom and anxious care. The summer was in its full beauty when she came down amongst us once more. Then the crushing blow came. Great doctors came from England and France; they lingered long before they gave their decision, but it came at length.

My mother might live for years, but she would never walk again; the flying feet were stilled for the rest of her life. She was to be a hopeless, helpless cripple. She might lie on the sofa, be wheeled in a chair, perhaps even driven in a carriage, but nothing more—she would never walk again.

My father's heart almost broke. I can see him now crying and sobbing like a child. He would not believe it. He turned from one to the other, crying out:

"It cannot be true! I will not believe it! She is so young and so beautiful—it cannot be true!"

"It is most unfortunately true," said the head physician, sorrowfully. "The poor lady will dance and walk no more."

"Who is to tell her?" cried my father. "I dare not."

"It will be far better that she should not know—a hundred times better. Let her live as long as she can in ignorance of her fate; she will be more cheerful and in reality far better than if she knew the truth; it would hang over her like a funeral pall; the stronger her nerve and spirit the better for her. She would regain neither, knowing this."

"But in time—with care—she is so young. Perhaps there may be a chance."

"I tell you plainly," said the doctor, "that most unfortunately there is none—there is not the faintest," and, he added, solemnly, "may Heaven lighten your afflictions to you!"

They went away, and my father drew me to his arms.

"Laura," he said, "you must help me all your life to take care of mamma."

"I will, indeed," I cried. "I ask nothing better from Heaven than to give my life to her—my beautiful mother."

And then he told me that she would never walk again—that her flying feet were to rest forever more—that in her presence I must always be quite bright and cheerful, and never say one word of what I knew.

No more difficult task could have been laid on the heart of a child. I did it. No matter what I suffered, I always went into her room with a smile and bright, cheerful words.

So the long years passed; my beautiful mother grew better and happier and stronger—little dreaming that she was never to walk out in the meads and grounds again. She was always talking about them and saying where she should go and what she should do when she grew well.

Roses bloomed, lilies lived and died, the birds enjoyed their happy summer, then flew over the sea to warmer climes; summer dew and summer rain fell, the dead leaves were whirled in the autumn winds, and still my mother lay helpless. If this one year seemed so long, what would a lifetime be?

As some of her strength returned it seemed to me that mother grew more and more charming. She laughed and enjoyed all our care of her, and when the wonderful chair came from London, in which she could go round the garden, and could be wheeled from one room to another, she was as delighted as a child.

"Still," she said to my father, "it seems to me a pity almost, Roland, to have sent to London for this. I shall surely be able to walk soon."

He turned away from her with tears in his eyes.

A month or two afterward we were both sitting with her, and she said, quite suddenly:

"It seems a long time since I began to lie here. I am afraid it will be many months before I get well again. I think I shall resign myself to proper invalids' fashions. I will have some pretty lace caps, Laura, and we will have more books." Then a wistful expression crossed her face and she said: "I would give anything on earth to walk, even only for ten minutes, by the side of the river; as I lie here I think so much about it. I know it in all its moods—when the wind hurries it and the little wavelets dash along; when the tide is deep and the water overflows among the reeds and grasses; when it is still and silent and the shadows of the stars lie on it, and when the sun turns it into a stream of living gold, I know it well."

"You will see it again soon," said my father, in a broken voice. "I will drive you down any time you like."

But my mother said nothing. I think she had seen the tears in Sir Roland's eyes. From that day she seemed to grow more reconciled to her lot. Now let me add a tribute to my father. His devotion to her was something marvelous; he seemed to love her better in her helpless state than he had done when she was full of health and spirits. I admired him so much for it during the first year of my mother's illness. He never left her. Hunting, shooting, fishing, dinner parties, everything was given up that he might sit with her.

One of the drawing rooms, a beautiful, lofty apartment looking over the park to the hills beyond, was arranged as my mother's room; there all that she loved best was taken.

The one next to it was made into a sleeping room for her, so that she should never have to be carried up and down stairs. A room for her maid came next. And my father had a door so placed that the chair could be wheeled from the rooms through the glass doors into the grounds.

"You think, then," she said, "that I shall not grow well just yet, Roland?"

"No, my darling, not just yet," he replied.

What words of mine could ever describe what that sick room became? It was a paradise of beautiful flowers, singing birds, little fragrant fountains and all that was most lovely. After a time visitors came, and my mother saw them; the poor came, and she consoled them.

"My lady" was with them once more, never more to walk into their cottages and look at the rosy children. They came to her now, and that room became a haven of refuge.

So it went on for three years, and I woke up one morning to find it was my thirteenth birthday.

## CHAPTER V.

That day both my parents awoke to the fact that I must have more education. I could not go to school; to have taken me from my mother would have been death to both of us. They had a long conversation, and it was decided that the wisest plan would be for me to have a governess—a lady who would at the same time be a companion to my mother. I am quite sure that at first she did not like it, but afterward she turned to my father, with a sweet, loving smile.

"It will relieve you very much," she said, "and give you time to get out."

"I shall never leave you," he said, "no matter who comes."

Several letters were written; my father gave himself unheard-of trouble; and after some weeks of doubt, hesitation and correspondence, a governess was selected for me. She had been living with Lady Bucarest, and was most highly recommended; she was amiable, accomplished, good tempered and well qualified for the duties Lady Tayne wished her to fulfill.

"What a paragon!" cried my father, as he read through the list of virtues.

"I hope we shall not be disappointed," said my mother. "Oh, Laura, darling, if it could be, I would educate you entirely, and give you into no other hands."

It was March when my governess—by name Miss Sara Reinhart—came. I always associate her in my own mind with the leaden skies, the cold winds, the bleak rains and biting frosts of March. She was to be with us on the seventh, and the whole of the day was like a tempest; the wind blew, the rain fell. We could hear the rustling of the great boughs; the wind rolled down the great avenues and shook the window frames.

My mother's room that day was the brightest in the house; cheery fire in the silver grate and the profusion of flowers made it so cheerful. How many times during that day both my father and mother said:

"What an uncomfortable journey Miss Reinhart will have!"

She ordered a good fire to be lighted in her bedroom and tea to be prepared for her. The carriage was sent to the station with plenty of wraps, and every care was taken of the strange lady. The wind was rolling like thunder through the great avenues, the tall trees bent under the fury of the blast; when the sound ceased I heard the carriage wheels, and going to my mother, who was reading, I said: "She has come."

My mother took my hand silently. Why did we both look at each other? What curious foreboding came to us both, that made us cling to each other? Poor mother! poor child!

Some time afterward my father came in and said:

"Will you see Miss Reinhart to-night, Beatrice, darling?"

She looked flushed and tired, but she answered, laughing quietly at her own nervousness:

"I suppose I shall not sleep unless I do see her, Roland. Yes, when she has taken her tea and had time to make herself quite comfortable, I shall be pleased to see her."

Why did we mother and child, cling to each other as though some terrible danger were overtaking us? It struck me that there was some little delay, and my father remained with the strange lady.

We had talked about her and wondered what she would be like. I had always pictured her as a girl many years older than myself, but still a girl, with a certain consciousness and shyness about her. I had expected that she would stand in awe of my mother at first, and be, perhaps, impressed with the grandeur of Tayne Abbey. When the time came to say that Miss Reinhart would be glad to see Lady Tayne, and Sir Roland brought the strange lady into the room, I was silently in utter amaze. This was no school-girl, no half-conscious, half-shy governess, impressed and awe-struck. There floated, rather than walked, into the room a beautiful woman, with dark draperies falling gracefully around her, a beautiful, self-possessed woman, whose every motion was harmony. She looked straight at my mother; one quick glance of her dark eyes seemed to take in every detail of the fair face and figure on the couch. She held out her hand white as my mother's own, and said:

"I am grieved to find you so ill, Lady Tayne, I hope I may be of good service to you."

"Thank you," said my mother's sweet voice, as their hands for one moment met.

Then the beautiful dark face turned to me.

"And this is my pupil," she said. "I hope we shall be good friends."

I had an uneasy sense that she was patronizing us. I looked across at my father. He was watching her with keen admiration on his face. I—with a child's keen instinct—had drawn nearer to my mother, as though to protect her. Then Sir Roland placed a chair for Miss Reinhart near my mother's sofa. She thanked him with a smile, and took it with the grace of a duchess.

Her manner was perfect. To my mother, gentle and deferential; to my father, respectful, with just a dash of quiet independence; to me kind and loving. Looking at her critically, it was almost impossible to find a finer woman—her head was beautifully shaped, her hair raven black and smooth as satin, little ears like pretty pink shells, a beautiful face with dark, dreamy eyes, thick dark lashes, straight, dark brows, and a mouth that was, perhaps, the loveliest feature in her face. It was not tragical beauty, either, but comfortable and comfort loving; there was a beautiful dimple in her white chin—a wicked dimple, suggestive of fun and laughter; another, and even more beautiful dimple, deepened near her lips, and laughed when she laughed. There was nothing of tragedy about her.

Very soon she was leading the conversation, telling us the details of her journey, but all in so humorous a fashion that it was quite irresistible. Sir Roland laughed as I had never seen him laugh before, and my mother was much amused. Any one looking on at the time would never have thought this was a governess undergoing a scrutiny, but rather a duchess trying to entertain her friends.

After some few minutes I saw my mother's sweet face grow pale, and I knew that she felt tired.

"Papa," I cried, forgetting my governess, "mamma is tired; look at her face."

Miss Reinhart rose at once and seemed to float to the sofa. "I am afraid," she said, "that I deserve rebuke. I was so anxious to cheer you that I fear I have tired you. Shall I take Miss Laura with me, or would you like to have her a little longer?"

My mother grasped my hand. "You are very kind," she said to Miss Reinhart, "but I am weak and nervous; so little tires me."

"Yes, it is very sad," she answered, in cold, sweet tones.

I hated her voice, I hated her sweetness, I hated her. Child as I was, a tempest of scorn and grief and bitter rebellion raged within me. Why should she stand there in what seemed to me the insolent pride of her beauty, while my sweet mother was never to stand again? Why should she speak in those pitying tones? My mother did not need her pity. Then my father came up, too, and said that Miss Reinhart had better delay for a few days before beginning the routine of her duties so as to get used to the place. She seemed quite willing.

"Laura," said Sir Roland, "will you take Miss Reinhart to her room?"

But I clung to my mother's hand.

"I cannot leave mamma," I said. "Please do not ask me."

He turned from me with an apology.

"Laura can never leave her mother," he said.

She answered:

"Laura is quite right."

But I caught just one glimpse of her beautiful eyes, which made me thoughtful.

She went, and my father was quite silent for some minutes afterward. Then my mother asked:

"What do you think of her, Roland?"

"Well, my darling, she is really so different to what I had expected, I can hardly form a judgment. I thought to see a crude kind of girl.

Miss Reinhart is a very beautiful woman of the world, as graceful, well-bred and self-possessed as a duchess."

"She is not half so beautiful as mamma," I cried.

"No, little faithful heart; not one-half," said Sir Roland.

"I must say that she seems to me far more like a fine lady visitor than a governess," said my mother.

"You will find her all right," said Sir Roland, brightly. "She seems to understand her duties and to be quite competent for them. I fancy you will like her Beatrice, darling; after all, it will be some thing to have some one to amuse us. How well she tells a story! with what brilliancy and verve!"

"I want no more amusement than I find with you and Laura," said my mother. "You are all-sufficient to me. Still, as you say, dear, it is well to have a pleasant companion."

Then, as my mother was tired, her maid came, and Sir Roland said, "Good-night."

I remember how we both felt sad and lonely, though we could not quite tell why; and that my beautiful mother fell fast asleep, holding my hand in hers; and that they would not take me away, lest they should awake her.

"And my lady has so little sleep," they said, pityingly, "we never awake her."

I wish, my darling, that for both of us it had been the long, sweet sleep from which there is no awaking.

## CHAPTER VI.

The first three days following Miss Reinhart's arrival were a holiday. My father himself showed her over the house, took her through the picture galleries, told her all the legends of the place. She walked out in the grounds and had learned to make herself quite at home. Sir Roland told her that she must do so, that her duties and responsibilities would be great. She must therefore take care of herself.

I was with them in the picture gallery, and Sir Roland never stopped to think that it would perhaps be better not to discuss such things before me.

"I hope," he said, "to interest you in the whole place. I cannot tell you how different things are when the mistress of the house is ill and helpless."

"I am sure it must be so," she said, in that sweet voice, which I felt to be false and hated.

"At any time," he said, "if you see things going wrong I should be grateful for a little management on your part."

"I will always do my very best for you, Sir Roland," she said, earnestly, and I could feel in some vague way that she was sympathizing with him and pitying him in a way that was against my mother's interests. I could hardly tell how.

"Have you a good housekeeper?" she asked, and my father answered:

"Mrs. Eastwood has been here over fifty years, I believe."

"Ah!" said Miss Reinhart, "that is too long; those very old housekeepers are faithful, and all that kind of thing, but they are seldom of much use. If everything does not go on as you wish in this unfortunate state of things, rely upon it that is what is wrong. You should pension this good Mrs. Eastwood off, and get some one young and active, with a thorough knowledge of her business."

"We will talk about it later on," he said. "I have no doubt but that you are quite right."

She looked up into his face with tender anxiety; I saw the look, and could have killed her for it.

"You know that I am devoted to your interests." she said. "I will cheerfully and gladly do everything and anything I can," she said, "to help you. You know you may command my services when and how you will."

She spoke with the air of a grandduchess offering to obtain court patronage, and my father made her a low, sweeping bow.

Who was she, that she should talk to my father of "unfortunate circumstances," and of her devotion to him? As for things going wrong, it was not true—my mother, from her sofa, ordered the household, and I knew there was nothing wrong.

When my father saw the angry, pained expression on my face, an idea seemed to occur to him. He called me to his side, and whispered to me:

"You may run away and play, darling; and mind, Laura, you must never repeat one word of what you hear to your mother; it would not do to trouble her when little things go wrong."

"Nothing has gone wrong," I answered. "Although she is ill, mamma sees to everything."

I should have said much more, but that my father placed his hand over my mouth.

"Hush! little one," he said. "I am afraid I give you too much license."

"A little wholesome discipline needed," said Miss Reinhart; "but a sweet child, Sir Roland—a sweet child, indeed!"

I could not hear what followed, but I feel quite sure that she whispered something which ended in these words:

"Too much with Lady Tayne."

I ran, fast as I could go, anywhere—where I could give vent to my childish fury. I could have stamped on her beautiful face. What right had she, a stranger, to talk about Mrs. Eastwood and mamma—to talk to papa as though he were an injured man—what right? I tried hard to keep all my indignation and anger, my fear and dread of what was to follow, to myself, but I could not bear it. I believe my heart would have broken but for Emma, my nurse. She found me behind the great cluster of laurel trees crying bitterly; and when she took me in her arms to console me, I told her all about it—told her every word. I know how she listened in dismay, for her easy, bony face grew pale, and she said nothing for some few minutes, then she cried out:

"Oh, Miss Laura, you must be good and patient; don't set yourself against her—perhaps she means no harm."

"She means harm and she will do it," I cried; "why should she speak in that tone to papa, and why does she look at him as though he were to be pitied because mamma is ill? It is mamma who wants pity; she is twenty times better lying there sick and ill than other mothers who are well and strong and go about everywhere."

"God bless the child!" cried my nurse; "why of course she is. Now, Miss Laura, you know I love you, and what I say to you is always because I do love you. Do what I say. You see she has to live here, and you had better try to make the best of it."

"She hates mamma and she hates me," I cried, unreasonably.

"Now, my dear little lady," said Emma, "how can you possibly know that? You are not reasonable or patient; try to make the best of it. It is of no use for you to make an enemy of the new lady; if you do I am sure you will suffer for it."

"Oh, Emma!" I cried, "why did she come; we were all so happy; we were all three so happy—why did she come? I did not want any education, I am sure."

"Pardon me, Miss Laura, but I think you do," said Emma, gravely.

"The only thing I want to live for at all is to be with mamma," I said—"to take care of her and try to make her happy. I do not want any other life than that."

"But," said my nurse, and I have often thought since what sense lay in her words, "do you know, Miss Laura, that my lady, who is so clever herself, will want an educated companion? For her sake you must learn all you can."

Those words gave me quite a new light. Why, of course I must; my mother was not only well educated, but she was also highly accomplished; she spoke French and German and had a very fair knowledge of Italian, whereas I had only just mastered the rudiments of English. New life, new ideas, new ambitions suddenly awoke within me, and, seeing her advantage, Emma pursued it.

"I have heard," she said, "that my lady is wonderfully clever. You will be her companion and her constant comfort; you must know some of the things she does. Now, Miss Laura, make up your mind, dear; instead of making the lady your enemy, be quick and learn all she can teach you—the sooner you know it all the sooner she will go."

Ah, that was something like a reason for studying; I would learn lessons all day and all night to insure her going. It must be a matter of years, but if by constant application I could shorten the time, even by one year, that was much. Then Emma gave me much sensible advice; above all, never to speak to mamma about Miss Reinhart.

"You see, Miss Laura, if your dear mamma took curious fancies against this lady, how dreadful it would be. It would make her much worse, and we do not know what might happen. Whatever occurs, bear it all patiently or come to me."

"My life is spoiled," I cried; "but I will do what you say."

And I made to myself a vow, which I kept through all temptation, never once to complain to my mother about Miss Reinhart. I did keep it, and Heaven knows how much it cost me. My father was rather surprised the next day when I went to his study and asked him if I could begin my lessons at once. He laughed.

"What an energetic scholar," he cried. "Why do you wish to begin so soon, Laura?"

"Because I have so very much to learn," I replied.

"You shall begin this day, Laura," he said; "but Miss Reinhart must see mamma first, and arrange the best hours for study. There are two or three little arrangements I should like changing—for instance, now that mamma is never present, I cannot see why you and Miss Reinhart should not take breakfast with me. I am very lonely, and should be delighted if we could manage that. But I must speak to mamma. Then I should like you to go on dining with me, as you have done since mamma's illness. It makes me quite ill to enter that great, desolate dining room. Do you remember how mamma's sweet face used to shine there, Laura?"

Did I? Did I ever enter the room without?

"Make your mind easy, Laura; you shall begin your lessons to-day, and we will see what mamma wishes to be done."

That day an arrangement was made: Miss Reinhart and I were to breakfast and dine with papa; the morning, until two was to be devoted to my studies, and the rest of the day, if mamma desired her presence, Miss Reinhart was to spend with her. We were to walk together, and I was, as usual, to go out with mamma when her chair was wheeled into the grounds.

"Heaven send that it may last!" said Emma, when she heard of it.

I wonder if any angel repeated the prayer?

## CHAPTER VII.

To me it seemed that I was as old at fifteen as many a girl of eighteen; I had lived so much with grown-up people; I had received all my impressions from them. I was very quick and appreciative. I read character well, and seemed to have a weird, uncanny insight into the thoughts and ideas of people—into their motives and plans. I had too much of this faculty, for I was often made uncomfortable because shadows came between me and others, and because I seemed to feel and understand things that I could never put into words.

Here is one little instance of what I mean: I stood one afternoon at the window of my mother's room. The sun was shining brightly on the bloom of countless flowers and the feathery spray of the fountains; the whole place looked so bright and beautiful that it was a perfect picture. I saw Miss Reinhart on the terrace; she was leaning over the stone balustrade admiring the magnificent view. There was a restless, disconsolate expression mixed with her admiration, and I knew quite well the thoughts passing through her mind were, first, a vivid regret that the place was not hers, then a wonder as to the possibility of its ever belonging to her. I could read it in the lingering, loving glance she threw round, followed by the impatient frown and restless movement. The idea possessed me so strongly that I could not help going to my mother and clasping my arms round her neck, as though I would save her from all harm; but I did not tell her why. I had learned my lesson; from first to last never a word passed my lips that could have grieved her even in the least, never.

The first thing that struck me in the manner of Miss Reinhart was the way in which she spoke to my father. Now, I am quite sure, no matter what came afterward, that at that time my father was one of the most loyal and honest of men. I am sure that he loved my mother with greatest affection: that her illness made her all the more dear to him, and that he looked upon it as a trial equally great for both of them; he loved her the more for it, and he devoted himself to her to make up to her as much as he could for the privations that she had to undergo. As for pitying himself, such an idea never occurred to him;

of that I am certain. All his love, pity, his compassion and sympathy, were for her, without any thought of himself; but she almost spoke to him as though he were to be pitied, as though he were very much injured and put upon, as though my mother's illness were a wrong done to him.

At first I noticed that he, too, seemed somewhat surprised; that he would look half-wonderingly at her; then, at last, he fell into her mood. She generally began at the breakfast table, where she came looking as beautiful as a picture; the loveliest hue of the rose on her face, the freshness of the morning in her dark eyes and on her lips; dressed with great elegance, always with one lovely flower in her hair, and a knot of fresh, fragrant blossoms at her breast; the fairest of women, but how I disliked her. I can imagine that to any gentleman her society must have been extremely agreeable.

My father's lonely breakfasts had often been a cause of great distress to him. He was essentially so gay and cheery; he loved the sound of voices and laughter; he liked to be amused; to discuss the plans for the day; to comment upon the letters received. To breakfast alone, or sit alone, was for him a torture; he sighed always when the breakfast bell rang, and we knew that it was a torture in its way. When my mother found it out she insisted upon my joining him every morning. I was but a child, and could not interest him very much.

Now the matter was quite different. There was Miss Reinhart, fresh and beautiful as the morning, witty and graceful, ready to ply him with flatteries, making tea for him with her own white hands, talking in the very brightest and most animated style. She had brilliant powers of conversation, and no one could be more amusing. Although I hated her, I often found myself hanging on the words that fell from her lips.

No wonder that the breakfast hour was prolonged, and that, often after the urn had grown cold, my father would cry out that he wanted more tea. Miss Reinhart arranged his papers for him; she laid them ready to his hand; they discussed the politics and the principal events of the day.

Young as I was, I was struck with her animation and verve. She spoke with such vivacity; her splendid face lighted with earnest, graceful enthusiasm. She held very original and clever ideas about everything, and it often happened that the conversation was prolonged until my father would take out his watch and exclaim with wonder at the time. Then Miss Reinhart would blush, and, taking me by the hand, disappear. More than once my father followed us, and, taking my hand, would say:

"Let us have a walk on the terrace before the lessons begin, Laura — Miss Reinhart will come with us."

But it was not to me he talked.

In the early days of her arrival I heard my dear mother once, when my father was speaking of her fine manners, say:

"We ought to be proud to have so grand a lady for governess."

Poor mamma, who knows the price she paid for a lady governess?

It was when these morning visits grew so long that I first began to notice the tone in which Miss Reinhart spoke of my mother.

She would lean her beautiful head just a little forward, her eyes bright with sweetest sympathy, her voice as beautifully sweet as the cooing of the ring-dove.

"How is dear Lady Tayne this morning, Sir Roland?" she would ask.

"I am afraid there is little difference and no improvement," was his reply.

"Ah, how sad — what a sad fate — so young and so afflicted. It must be dreadful for you, Sir Roland. I sympathize so much with you. I never quite lose sight of your troubles. I do not know that there could possibly be a greater one."

At first my father would laugh, and say gently:

"Ah, yes, there could be one — it would be so much worse if my dear wife had died."

But after a time he began to shake his head gravely as she shook hers, and sigh as he answered:

"Ah, yes, it is a terrible infliction."

If any little domestic unpleasantness occurred, a thing by Sir Roland's desire always kept from my mother, she would look so kindly at him.

"Dear Sir Roland, how tiresome all this is for you. I wonder you are so patient." Could my mother help it, I cried to myself with passionate tears; was it her fault that she was stricken and helpless; ought this woman to speak to my father about it as though he were the sufferer? The tears that fell from my eyes blinded me; thus I had to go to my lessons, my heart torn with its sense of injury and resentment against the one who seemed to me my mother's enemy, I knew not why.

Again, if there was a question about any visitors, and my father seemed at a loss for a few minutes, she would say:

"How painful it is for you, Sir Roland, to be troubled in this fashion; can I do anything to help you?" Or it would be, "How sorry I am to see you teased about such trifles, Sir Roland; can I manage it for you?"

The same when he received invitations: before now it had seemed at least almost a pleasure to decline them. I could remember how he used to take both the letters of invitation and his refusals and send them to my mother, commenting on them as he read. That was always followed by a pretty little love scene, during which my mother would express her regret that he was deprived of a pleasure; and he always answered that the only pleasure he had was to be with her.

Nor do I believe that state of things would ever have changed but for Miss Reinhart. Now, when these letters came and he would read them with knitted brow, she would inquire gently, ah, and with such sweet, seductive sweetness, if anything in his letters had put him out.

"No," he would answer with a sigh. "Oh, no! There is nothing in my letters to annoy me—just the contrary. I ought to feel delighted. Sir Charles Pomfret wishes me to go over to Pomfort Castle for a few days; he has a fine large party there, and several of my old friends among them."

"What a disappointment to you," she cried. "You must feel these things sorely."

A frown instead of a smile passed over his face.

I remember when he used to laugh, and say that it was a pleasure to give up anything to be with my mother. Now he began to pace up and down the room while she looked after him with pitiful eyes. Suddenly she rose, and, going up to him, laid her hand on his arm. She gazed earnestly into his face.

"Why stay away, Sir Roland? I am sure you might go if you would. I will take care of Lady Tayne. I do not see that you need be anxious, or that there is the least need for giving up the party; let me persuade you to go."

"It seems unkind to leave Lady Tayne," he said. "I have never left her for so long, and never alone."

"If you will trust her to me, I will take the greatest care of her," said Miss Reinhart; "and I am sure, quite sure, that if Lady Tayne knew, she would insist on it—she would indeed. She would be the last to wish you to give up every pleasure for her sake."

It was the thin end of the wedge, but she succeeded in driving it in.

He went. It was the first time he had left my mother, but by no means the last. He went himself to tell her that he had decided on going. She was most amiable and unselfish, and told him what was perfectly true—that she was delighted, and that if he would begin to go out without her she would be most happy. I know that she was unselfishly glad, yet her sweet face was paler that night than usual; and once more I felt sure that there were tears in her eyes.

My father's visit was prolonged for a whole week, and very much he enjoyed it. He wrote home every day; but it did not seem natural to me that Miss Reinhart should be waiting for him in the hall, or that he should tell her all about his visit long before he went to my mother's room.

But it was so, and my poor, dear mother did not know it.

## CHAPTER VIII.

The first real rebellion, and the first time that the eyes of people were opened to the amount of influence and authority that Miss Reinhart had acquired in Tayne Hall. One or two domestic matters had gone wrong—nothing very much, but dinner was late several times, and the household machinery did not seem to run on as it had done. My father complained; the cook did not evidently take so much pains.

"There is no one to look after her," he said, with a deep sigh.

Miss Reinhart responded by another.

"Dear Sir Roland, can I help you—may I help you?" she explained. "Your housekeeper is too old; you will never do any good until you have another."

"But," said my father, "she has been here so long; she was my mother's housekeeper long before I was born. It does not seem right to send away an old servant."

"You need not send her away, I said before; you might pension her off."

"I will speak to Lady Tayne about it. She has very peculiar ideas on that point. I must see what she thinks about it."

"Of course," said Miss Reinhart, "you will do as you think best, Sir Roland—and your way is, I am sure, always the best—but I should have thought, considering the very nervous state that Lady Tayne always lies in, that it would have been far better not to let her know about it until it is all over."

My father thought for a few moments, and then he said:

"No, I should not like to do that; it would seem like taking an unfair advantage of her helplessness."

Miss Reinhart blushed deeply.

"Oh, Sir Roland!" she cried, "you could not suppose that I thought of such a thing! I assure you I am quite incapable of it. I thought only of dear Lady Tayne."

And she seemed so distressed, so concerned and anxious that my father hardly knew how to reassure her. She explained and protested until at last, and with something of impatience, he said:

"I will speak to Lady Tayne about it this morning." I knew he felt in want of some kind of moral support when he took my hand and said, in would-be careless words: "Come with me, Laura, to see mamma."

And we went, hand-in-hand, to my mother's room. There, after the usual loving greetings had been exchanged, my father broached the subject which evidently perplexed and sadly worried him. Broached it ever so gently, but I, who knew every look and trick of my mother's face, saw how deeply pained she was. She never attempted to interrupt him, but when he had finished speaking — having passed over very lightly indeed the little domestic matters which had gone wrong since my mother's illness, dwelling principally upon the benefit that would most probably accrue if a younger housekeeper were engaged — my mother declined to do anything of the kind.

"My dear Roland," she said, "it would literally break my heart; think what a faithful old servant she has been."

"That is just it," said my father; "she is too old — too old, Miss Reinhart thinks, to do her work well."

There is a moment's silence.

"Miss Reinhart thinks so," said my mother, in those clear, gentle tones I knew so well; "but then, Roland, what can Miss Reinhart know about our household matters?"

That question puzzled him, for I believe that he himself was quite unconscious how or to what extent he was influenced by my governess.

"I should think," he replied, "that she must have noticed the little disasters and failures. She is only anxious to spare you trouble and help you."

"That would not help me, sending away an attached and faithful old servant like Mrs. Eastwood and putting a stranger in her place."

"But if the stranger should be more efficient of the two, what then, Beatrice?"

"I do not care about that," she said, plaintively. "Mrs. Eastwood could have an assistant—that would be better. You see, Roland, I am so accustomed to her, she knows all my ways, and sends me just what I like. I am so thoroughly accustomed to her I could not bear a stranger."

"But, my darling, the stranger would never come near you," said my father.

"Mrs. Eastwood does," said my mother. "You do not know, Roland, when my maid and nurse are tired she often comes to sit with me in the dead of night, and we can talk about old times, even before you were born. She tells me about your mother and you when you were a little boy. I should not like to lose her. Miss Reinhart does not understand."

"That settles the affair, my darling. If you do not decidedly wish it, it shall never be done."

She drew his face down to hers and kissed it.

"You are so good to me," she said, gently. "You bear so much for my sake. I know that you will not mind a little inconvenience every now and then. I am sure you will not."

"No; if you wish her to stay she shall do so," said Sir Roland; but I, who know every play of his features, feel quite sure that he was not pleased.

Little was said the next morning at breakfast time. Sir Roland said hurriedly that Lady Tayne did not wish to change; she was attached to the old housekeeper, and did not like to lose her. Miss Reinhart listened with a gentle, sympathetic face.

"Yes," she said, "it will, of course, be much more pleasant for Lady Tayne, but you should be considered as well. I know of a person, a most excellent, economical managing woman, who is competent in every way to undertake the situation. Still, if I cannot serve you in one way, can I not in another? Shall I try to make matters easier for

Mrs. Eastwood? I understand housekeeping very well. I could do some good, I think!"

"You are very kind to offer," he said. "I really do not like to complain to Lady Tayne. She cannot possibly help it, and it distresses her. Not that there is much the matter, only a few little irregularities; but then you will not have time."

"If you give me the permission," she said, "I will make the time."

"It would really be a kindness," he said, "and I am very grateful to you indeed. Perhaps you will be kind enough just to overlook matters for me."

I was with them, listening in fear and trembling, for I knew quite well that Mrs. Eastwood would never submit to the rule of my governess. No woman on earth ever played her cards so skillfully as Miss Reinhart. She did not begin by interfering with the housekeeping at once; that would not have been policy; she was far too wise.

She began by small reforms. The truth must be told. Since my mother's long illness our household had in some measure relaxed from its good discipline. At first Miss Reinhart only interfered with the minor arrangements. She made little alterations, all of which were conducive to my father's comfort, and he was very grateful. When he saw that she did so well in one direction, he asked her to help in another; and at last came, what I had foreseen, a collision with Mrs. Eastwood.

The Wars of the Roses were nothing to it. But for the pitiful tragedy embodied in it, I could have laughed as at a farce. Miss Reinhart was valiant, but Mrs. Eastwood was more valiant still. The whole household ranged itself on one side or the other. The old servants were all on the housekeeper's side, the new ones went with Miss Reinhart.

"A house divided against itself cannot stand." Ours did not. Before long the rival powers came into collision, and there was a declaration of war—war to the knife!

Miss Reinhart, "speaking solely in the interests of Sir Roland," wished the dinner hour to be changed; it would be more convenient and suitable to Sir Roland if it were an hour later. The housekeeper said that to make it an hour later would be to disturb all the arrangements of the house, and it could not be done.

Miss Reinhart said it was the duty of the housekeeper to obey.

The housekeeper said that she was accustomed to take her orders from the master and mistress of the house, and that she did not recognize that of the governess.

"You will be compelled to recognize mine, Mrs. Eastwood, if you remain here," she said.

"Then I shall not remain," said the old housekeeper, trembling with indignation, which was exactly what Miss Reinhart had desired her to say.

"You had better tell Sir Roland yourself," said my governess, in her cold, impassive manner. "It has nothing whatever to do with me. Sir Roland wishes me to attend to these things, and I have done so—the result does not lie with me."

"I have lived here, the most faithful and devoted of servants, for more than fifty years. Why should you turn me away, or seek to turn me away?" she said. "I have never wronged you. You may get one more clever, but no one who will love my lady as I do—no one who will serve her one-half so faithfully or so well, try your best, Miss Reinhart."

"I have nothing to do with it," she replied coldly. "I will tell Sir Roland that you desire to leave—there my business ends."

"I beg your pardon, Miss Reinhart, there it does not end. I have no wish to leave the place and family I love so well; but I say that I would rather leave than obey you."

"I will word your message just as you wish," she said; "there shall be no mistake."

I was with her when that conversation was repeated to Sir Roland, and I may say that was my first real experience in the real deceit of the world. Repeated to him, it bore quite a different aspect; it was an insolent rebellion against proper authority, and my father resented it very much.

"Unless you had told me yourself, I would not have believed it, Miss Reinhart."

"It is quite true," she replied, calmly, looking, in her exquisite morning dress, calm, sweet and unruffled as an angel.

I believe, honestly, that from that time she tried to make things worse. Every day the feud increased, until the whole household seemed to be ranged one against the other. If the housekeeper said one thing, Miss Reinhart at once said the opposite. Then an appeal would be made to Sir Roland, who gradually became worn and worried of the very sound of it.

"You will do no good," said Miss Reinhart to my father, "until you have pensioned that old housekeeper off. Once done, you will have perfect peace."

Constant dripping wears away a stone. My father was so accustomed to hearing she must go that at last the idea became familiar to him. I am quite sure that Miss Reinhart had made this her test; that she had said to herself—if she had her own way in this, she should in everything else. It was her test of what she might do and how far she might go.

It came at last. The blow fell on us, and she won. My father spoke seriously to my mother. He said Mrs. Eastwood could have a cottage on the estate, and he should allow her a sufficient income to live upon. She could come to the Abbey when she liked to call on my mother, and might be as happy as possible. It was not just to the other servants, or even to themselves, he said, to keep one in such a position who was really too old to fulfill the duties.

My mother said nothing. It must be just as my father pleased. But when he added that Miss Reinhart thought it the best thing possible, she turned away her face and said no more.

## CHAPTER IX.

How the shadow fell, I cannot quite remember—how people first began to find out there was something wrong at Tayne Hall. Mrs. Eastwood, after a long interview with my mother, had gone away to the cottage, and Miss Reinhart had brought some person, whom she appeared to know very well, on the scene.

Many of the servants would believe that the new housekeeper was the governess' mother—there was a certain similarity of face and figure between them; whether it was so or not, mattered little. From the hour that Mrs. Stone entered the house my dear mother's rule may be said to have ended; from that time domestic management may be summed up in a few words—constant opposition to my mother's wishes and constant, flattering attention to those of my father. If my mother missed the little dainties that Mrs. Eastwood had lavished on her, my father appreciated to the full the comfortable arrangements, the punctuality over dinner, the bright and fresh appearance of everything. Nor was Miss Reinhart slow in reminding him that he owed all this extra comfort to her selection of a good housekeeper.

It was but natural to suppose that Mrs. Stone looked upon the governess as the highest authority in the house after Sir Roland; she never appealed or applied to any one else; she never, I should say, even remembered the existence of my mother. As for any reference to her, she never thought of it. Hundreds of times, when I have been busy with my lessons, she has come to the study, and, rapping at the door, has asked to speak to my governess. I could hear her plainly saying: "Do you think Sir Roland would like this?" And they would consult most eagerly about it. I never once heard my name mentioned.

"Miss Reinhart," I asked her one morning. "Why do you never think or speak of my mother? Mrs. Stone never inquires what she would like."

In the blandest tone of voice she replied to me:

"My dear Laura, children—and you are but a child—should not ask such questions."

"I am a very old child," I replied, with a sigh. "But whether I am a child or not, I can see that very little attention is ever paid to my mother."

"Has Lady Tayne complained?" she asked, hurriedly.

"No, and never will," I replied, with all a child's pride in a mother's courage.

"I thought as much," she said, with a peculiar smile. "Lady Tayne has plenty of sense."

"She has plenty of patience," I replied, "and plenty of opportunity of exercising it."

"So much the better," replied Miss Reinhart, and then we resumed our lessons.

It was soon all over with the old servants. I wonder that my father, so sensible, so keen in other matters, could not see that her sole ambition was to have every person in the house under her control. One by one the old servants disappeared—there was some fault or other with each one—and my father grew more passive at each attack, and made less resistance; he was so deeply impressed with the fact that every change resulted in greater comfort for himself.

One morning when, by some rare chance, I was left alone with Sir Roland, and the faces of strange servants passed in and out:

"Papa," I said, "we have great changes in the house."

"Yes," he replied, brightly; "and so far as I can see, they have conduced greatly to our benefit."

"I want you to grant me one favor, papa—will you?"

"Certainly, my Laura," he replied. "Why, what does this mean?" for I had thrown myself in his arms with passionate tears—"what is this, Laura?"

"I want you to promise me," I said, "that, whatever changes go on, you will not let any one send mamma's maid, Patience, away?"

He looked dreadfully shocked.

"Your mother's maid, child?" he said. "Why, who dare even suggest such a thing? Certainly not. The whole household is constructed with a view to your mother's happiness."

So she had told him, and so he believed. It was quite useless talking; he did not see, he did not, indeed.

I knew Emma disliked her and Patience, too. The farce of her being my mother's companion was very soon played out. She never came near, unless my father went, and then she did not remain long. But— and we, the three who loved her, noted it with dismay—every day Miss Reinhart became more of a companion to my father. She ingratiated herself by degrees. At first it had been merely his breakfast, afterward she offered her services over his letters; she answered many of them in a clear, legible hand that pleased him, because it was so easily read. Then his accounts. I went in several times and found them seated at the table, side by side, with papers, ledgers and books, yet not so deeply engrossed but that every now and then they had a jest and a merry laugh.

Did he think of my mother during those hours? Did her pale, sweet, wistful face ever come between him and that beautiful woman?

Then I noticed that he would say to her:

"Come out for a few minutes, Miss Reinhart, out on the terrace here, and let us have some fresh air. If you will permit me, I will smoke my cigar. Will you come, Laura?"

I suppose it was natural; she was a beautiful woman, full of talent and animation, brilliant and fascinating, only too anxious to please him in every way, laying herself out to captivate him, and he never could endure being alone.

Ah, me! what my childish heart suffered—of rage, and terror, and pain—when I saw my mother's eyes turned wistfully to the door, waiting, watching for him and asking me, in the sweet, low tones, if I knew where he was. I learned my lesson sharply enough. The first time she asked me one bright, sunny morning, when she seemed a little better, and had a great desire to go out.

"I wish papa would go with me, Laura," she said. "I never enjoy anything without him. Where is he?"

I had seen him ten minutes before that on the lower terrace with Miss Reinhart, and they were going to the grounds. He was smoking a cigar; she was looking most fascinating and beautiful in her elegant morning dress and coquettish hat. Without thinking, I replied, hastily:

"He is out in the grounds with Miss Reinhart."

Ah, heaven! shall I ever forget the face turned to mine, so white, so scared, so stricken?

"What did you say, Laura? Come here; I did not hear you."

Then, when her trembling hands clutched mine, I knew what I had done quite well. Patience came round to my mother with a look at me that spoke volumes.

"My lady," she said, "do pray be calm. You know how ill even the least emotion makes you, and Miss Laura is so frightened when you are ill!"

The sweet face grew whiter.

"I will remember," she said.

Then she repeated the question, but my intelligence had grown in the last few minutes.

"Papa is out in the grounds," I replied, "and I saw him speaking to Miss Reinhart."

"But," said my mother, "your papa does not walk out with Miss Reinhart. Laura, darling, you must think before you speak."

Now, I knew that Sir Roland went out every day with my governess; more than that, two or three times each day I had seen them; but Patience looked at me with a solemn warning in her face, and I answered, as I kissed her:

"I will try, darling mother. Shall I ever speak as plainly and as prettily as you do, I wonder?"

I loved to make little loving, flattering speeches to her, they pleased her so much and brightened her sweet face; but that evening, when I went back to her room, I saw her eyes were swollen with weeping. I vowed to myself to be careful.

"Where is papa, darling?" she asked, with loving, wistful eyes. "I have only seen him once to-day."

"He is still in the dining-room, mamma." Then I added, with a guilty, blushing face, for I had left my governess with him, "and you know that I am growing wise enough to understand gentlemen like a nod over the last glass of port."

"And Miss Reinhart, Laura, where is she?"

I was so unused to speaking anything but the plain, simple truth—it was an effort even to evade the question, and say that she generally enjoyed herself after dinner in her own fashion. She looked very relieved, and Patience gave me a friendly nod, as though she would say, "You are improving, Miss Laura."

Even after that, so soon as I entered the room, the loving, wistful eyes would seek mine, and the question was always on her lips:

"Where is papa?"

One night she did not seem so well. I was startled myself by the march of events—for Patience came to the drawing-room door, where Sir Roland and Miss Reinhart were sitting, and looked slightly confused, as she said:

"I have taken the liberty of coming to you, Sir Roland. You wished me always to tell you when my lady was not so well—she seems very depressed and lonely."

"I will go and sit with Lady Tayne," he said.

Then he glanced at the beautiful, brilliant face of Sara Reinhart.

"Laura, why are you not sitting with your mother to-night?"

And I dare not tell him that my jealous heart would not let me leave him alone with her.

I understood that night the art with which she managed him, and with it—child though I was—I had a feeling of contempt for the weak nature so easily managed.

He came back to her looking confused.

"We must defer our game at chess, Miss Reinhart," he said. "Lady Tayne is not so well; I am going to sit with her. Come on, Laura."

"How good you are, Sir Roland," she said, impulsively. "You are so self-sacrificing. I must follow your good example. Can I go to the library and find a book? The evenings are very long."

He looked irresolutely at her.

"You must find them very long," he said. "I am very sorry."

"It cannot be helped," she answered. "I have always heard that the nights in the country were twice as long as those in town. I believe it."

I knew by instinct what she meant; there was no need for words. It was a veiled threat that if my father did not spend his evenings with her she would go back to town. He knew it as well, I am sure, from the look on his face. I never like to think of that evening, or how it was spent by us in my mother's room.

## CHAPTER X.

When this unfortunate state of affairs in our household first became public property, I cannot tell. I saw the servants, some grow dissatisfied and leave, some grow impertinent, while some kind of mysterious knowledge was shared by all.

"Miss Laura," said my good nurse, Emma, to me one day, "I want to talk to you very seriously. You are fifteen, and you are no longer a child. I want to impress this much upon your mind—never say anything to your mamma about Miss Reinhart, and if my lady asks any questions, try to say as little as possible—do you understand?"

I looked at her. Of what use was concealment with this honest, loving heart?

"Yes," I said; "I quite understand Emma. You mean that I must never tell mamma anything about papa and—Miss Reinhart?"

"Heaven bless the child!" cried the startled woman; "you could not have understood better or more had you been twenty years old."

"It is love for mamma that teaches me that and everything else," I answered.

"Ah, well, Miss Laura, since you speak frankly to me, so will I to you. I would not say one word against Sir Roland for all the world. Before she came he was the kindest and most devoted of husbands; since she has been here he has changed, there is no doubt of it—terribly changed. My lady does not know all that we know. She thinks he is tired of always seeing her ill. She only suspects about Miss Reinhart, she is not sure, and it must be the work of our lives to keep her from knowing the truth."

"Emma," I ventured to interrupt, "do you think it is the truth?"

"Yes, I fear so; and, Miss Laura, you must bear one thing in mind, if ever my lady knows it to be the truth it will kill her. We must be most careful and always wear the brightest faces before her, and never let her know that anything is going wrong."

"I will do it always," I said, and then, looking up, I saw that my nurse was sad and grave. "How will it end, Emma?" I asked.

"Only God knows, miss," she replied. "One thing, I hope, is this— that my lady will never find it out."

Something was telling upon my dear mother every day; she grew thinner and paler; the sweet smile, sweet always, grew fainter; her face flushed at the least sound. Last year my father would have been devoured by anxiety; now his visits were short and cold. If I said one word my mother would interrupt me. "Hush! my Laura," she would say, gently; "gentlemen are not at home in a sick-room. Dear papa is all that is kind, but sitting long in one room is like imprisonment to him; I love him far too much to wish him to do it."

Then I would take the opportunity of repeating some kind word that I had heard my father say of her. But do as we would, the shadow fell deeper and darker every day.

The sense of degradation fell upon me with intolerable weight. That our household was a mark for slander—a subject of discussion, a blot on the neighborhood, I understood quite well; that my father was blamed and my mother pitied I knew also, and that Miss Reinhart was detested seemed equally clear. She was very particular about going to church, and every Sunday morning, whether Sir Roland went or not, she drove over to the church and took me with her. When I went with my mother I had always enjoyed this hour above all others. All the people we knew crowded around us and greeted us so warmly—every one had such pleasant things to say to us. Now, if a child came near where we stood, silent and solitary, it was at once called back. If Miss Reinhart felt it, she gave no indication of such feeling; only once—when three ladies, on their way to their carriages, walked the whole round of the church-yard rather than cross the path on which she stood—she laughed a cynical laugh that did not harmonize with the beauty of her face.

"What foolish, narrow-minded people these country people are!" she said.

"How do you measure a mind?" I asked, and she answered, impatiently, that children should not talk nonsense.

# My Mother's Rival

The worst seemed to have come now. Some of our best servants left. Three people remained true to my mother as the needle to the pole — myself, Emma and Patience; we were always bright and cheerful in her presence. I have gone in to see her when my heart has been as heavy as death, and when my whole soul has been in hot rebellion against the deceit practiced upon her, when I have shuddered at every laugh I forced from my lips.

She had completely changed during the last few months. All her pretty invalid ways had gone. There was no light in her smiles — they were all patience. She had quite ceased to ask about papa; where he was, what he was doing, or anything about him. He went to her twice a day — once in the morning and again at night. He would bend down carelessly and kiss her forehead; and tell her any news he had heard, or anything he fancied would interest her, and after a few minutes go away again. There was no more lingering by her couch or loving dislike to leaving her — all that was past and gone.

My mother never reproached him — unless her faithful love was a reproach. One thing I shall always hope and believe; it is this, that she never even dreamed in those days of the extent of the evil. The worst she thought was that my father encouraged Miss Reinhart in exceeding the duties of her position; that he had allowed her to take a place that did not belong to her, and that he permitted her to act in an intimate manner with him. She believed also that my father, although he still loved her and wished her well, was tired of her long illness, and consequently tired of her.

That was bad enough; but fortunately that was the worst just then — of deeper evil she did not dream; only we three, who loved her faithfully and well, knew that.

But matters were coming to a crisis. I was resting in the nursery one afternoon — my head had been aching badly — and Emma said an hour's sleep would take it away. She drew down the blinds and placed my head on the pillow.

There was deeper wrong with my heart than with my head.

My eyes closed, and drowsy languor fell over me. The door opened, and I saw Alice Young, a very nice, respectable parlor maid, who had not been with us long, enter the room.

51

"Hush!" said my nurse, "Miss Laura is asleep."

I was not quite, but I did not feel able to contradict them. What did it matter?

"I will not wake missie, but I want to speak to you," she said. "I am in great trouble, Emma. I have had a letter from my mother this morning, and she says I am to leave this place at once, that it is not respectable, and that people are talking of it all over the county. What am I to do?"

"Go, I suppose," said Emma.

The girl grew nearer to her.

"Do you think it is true?" she asked. "I saw him driving her out yesterday, and three days ago I saw his arm around her waist; but, still, do you really think it is true, Emma?"

"It does not matter to us," said Emma.

"Yes, it does matter," persisted the other. "If it is really true, this is no place for us; and if it be untrue, some one ought to put an end to it. I have nothing but my character, and if that goes, all goes. Now, I ask you to tell me, Emma, ought I to go or stay?"

My nurse was silent for some few minutes, then she said:

"You had better go. While missie and my lady stop here, I shall stay, and when they go, I go. My duty is to them."

Then I raised my white, miserable face from the pillow.

"Do not say any more," I cried. "I am not asleep, and I understand it all."

"Law, bless the dear young lady!" cried Alice, aghast. "I would not have spoken for the world if I had known" —

But I interrupted her.

"It does not matter, Alice," I said. "You meant no harm, and I am old in misery, though young in years."

The girl went away, and Emma flung herself on her knees before me.

"I am so sorry, Miss Laura," she began, "but I had not patience to listen—my heart was full of one thing."

"Emma," I said, "tell me, do you think mamma really knows or suspects any of these things?"

"No," was the quiet reply, "I do not. I will tell you why, Miss Laura. If my lady even thought so, she would not allow Miss Reinhart to remain in the house another hour with you."

"I am going to papa now, and I shall ask him to send my governess away," I said. "She shall not stop here."

## CHAPTER XI.

My father had always been kind to me—he had never used a harsh word to me. My heart was full—it was almost bursting—when I went to him. The shame, the degradation, the horror, were full upon me. Surely he would hear reason. I dared not stop to think. I hastened to him. I flung my arms round his neck and hid my face upon his breast. My passionate sobs frightened him at first.

"My dearest Laura, what is the matter?" he asked.

"Papa, send Miss Reinhart away," I cried; "do send her away. We were so happy before she came, and mamma was happy. Can you not see there is a black shadow hanging over the house? Send it away—be as you were before she came. Oh, papa, she has taken you from us."

When I told him what I had heard he looked shocked and horrified.

"My poor child! I had no idea of this."

He laid me on the couch while he walked up and down the room.

"Horrible!" I heard him say. "Frightful! Poor child! Alice shall go at once!"

He rang the bell when he had compelled me to repeat every word I had overheard, and sent for the housekeeper. I heard the whispering, but not the words—there was a long, angry conversation. I heard Sir Roland say "that Alice and every one else who had shared in those kind of conversations should leave." Then he kissed me.

"Papa," I cried to him, "will you send Miss Reinhart away? No other change is of any use."

"My dear Laura, you are prejudiced. You must not listen to those stupid servants and their vile exaggerations. Miss Reinhart is very good and very useful to me. I cannot send her away as I would dismiss a servant—nor do I intend."

"Let her go, that we may be happy as we were before. Oh, papa! she does not love mamma. She is not good; every one dislikes her. No one will speak to her. What shall we do? Send her away!"

"This is all a mistake, Laura," he said; "a cruel—I might say wicked—mistake. You must not talk to me in this way again."

Perhaps more might have been said; it might even have been that the tragedy had been averted but for the sudden rap at the door and the announcement that the rector wished to see Sir Roland.

"Ask him to step in here," said my father, with a great mark of discomposure. "Laura, run away, child, and remember what I have said. Do not speak to me in this fashion again."

I learned afterward that the rector had called to remonstrate with him—to tell him what a scandal and shame was spreading all over the country side, and to beg of him to end it.

Many hours elapsed before I saw my father again. I saw him ride out of the courtyard and did not see him return. When I had gone to his room in the morning I had taken with me one of my books, and I wanted it for my studies in the morning.

It was neither light nor dark. I went quietly along the broad corridors to my father's study. I never gave one thought to the fact that my father might be there. I had not seen him return. I went in. The study was a very long room with deep windows. Quite at the other end, with the firelight shining on his face, stood my father, and by his side Miss Reinhart, just as I had seen him stand with my beautiful mother a hundred times; one arm was thrown round her, and he was looking earnestly in her face.

"It must be so," he said; "there is no alternative now."

She clung to him, whispering, and he kissed her.

I stole away. Oh! my injured, innocent mother. I do not remember exactly what I did. I rushed from the house out into the great fir wood and wept out my hot, rebellious anger and despair there. At breakfast time the next morning just a gleam of hope came to me. Miss Reinhart said that, above everything else, she should like a drive.

Whether it was my pleading and tears or the rector's visit which had made my father think, I cannot tell, but for the first time he seemed quite unwilling to drive her out. The tears came into her eyes and he went over to her and whispered something which made her smile. He talked to her in a mysterious kind of fashion that I could neither understand nor make out at all—of some time in the future.

An uneasy sense of something about to happen came over me. I could feel the approach of some dark shadow; all day the same sensation rested with me, yet I saw nothing to justify it. At night my mother called me to her side.

"Laura, you do not look so cheerful this evening. What makes my daughter so sad?"

I could not tell her of that scene I had witnessed; I could not tell her of what was wrong.

On the morning following this, to me, horrible day, I could not help seeing that there was quite a new understanding between my father and Miss Reinhart. I overheard him say to her:

"It would have been quite impossible to have gone on; the whole country would have been in an uproar."

All that day there seemed to me something mysterious going on in the house; the servants went about with puzzled faces; there were whisperings and consultations. I heard Patience say to Emma:

"It is not true. I would not believe it. It is some foolish exaggeration of the servants. I am sure it is not true."

"Even if it should be I do not know what we could do," said Emma. "We cannot prevent it. If he has a mind to do such a bad action, he will do it, if not at one time, surely at another."

What was it? I never asked questions now.

One thing I remember. When I went into his room that evening to say good-night, my father's traveling flask lay there—a pretty silver flask that my mother had given him for a birthday present. He bade me "good-night," and I little thought when or how we should meet again.

## CHAPTER XII.

I do not judge or condemn him. I do not even say what I should say if he were any other than my father. His sin was unpardonable; perhaps his temptation was great; I cannot tell. The Great Judge knows best. I will tell my miserable story just as it happened.

The day following—another bright, sunny, warm morning, all sunshine, song and perfume, the birds singing so sweetly and the fair earth laughing. It was so bright and beautiful that when I went out into the grounds my troubles seemed to fade away. I hastened to gather some flowers for my mother; the mignonette was in bloom, and that was her favorite flower. I took them to her, and we talked for a few minutes about the beauty of the day. She seemed somewhat better, and asked me to get through my studies quickly, so that we might go through the grounds. I hastened to the school-room. Miss Reinhart was not there. I took my books and sat down by the window waiting for her. As I sat there, one after another the servants looked in the room, as though in search of something, then vanished. At last I grew tired of waiting, and rang to ask if Miss Reinhart was coming to give me my lessons. Emma came in reply.

Miss Reinhart would not be there yet, she said, and it would be better for me to go out now with my lady and to attend to my books afterward.

It struck me that every one seemed in a hurry to get us out of the house. Patience King was not to be seen, and Emma did not like to come near us because of her tear-stained face. Just as we were leaving the house my mother turned to the footman, who was at the back of her chair:

"John," she said, "go and ask Sir Roland if he will come with us."

I saw the man's face flush crimson, but he went away and returned in a few minutes, saying that his master was not in.

My mother repeated the words in some wonder.

"Have you seen papa this morning, Laura?"

"No; Emma brought my breakfast to me."

"I have not seen him either," she said. "He has not been to say good-morning to me yet. John, leave word that when Sir Roland comes in we shall be on the grass plot near the sun-dial!"

Why did they all look at us with such scared faces, with such wondering eyes? And I felt sure that I heard one say to the other:

"I have sent for the rector."

We went—as unconscious of the doom that hung over us as two children—went my mother's rounds. She looked at all the flowers, but turned to me once or twice and said, uneasily:

"I wonder where Sir Roland is? It seems strange not to have seen him."

We talked about him. There was nothing she liked more than speaking of him to me. We were out, I should think, at least three hours, and then my mother felt faint, and we went back.

The good rector met us and shook hands very kindly with us, but he was pale and agitated, not like himself in the least. Patience was there, and Emma; the other servants were huddled in groups, and I knew something very terrible had happened—something—but what?

The rector said Lady Tayne was tired, and must have some wine. My mother took it, and was placed upon her couch once more. She turned to the footman and asked if my father had returned. The answer was—no. Then the rector said he wished to speak to her alone. He held a letter in his hands, and his face was as pale as death. She looked up at him and said, quickly:

"Is it bad news?"

"Yes," he answered, gravely; "it is very bad news. Laura, go away and leave your mother with me."

But my mother clung to me.

"No, if I have anything to suffer," she cried, "let Laura stay with me— I can bear anything with her."

"Let me stay?" I asked.

He covered his face with his hands, and was silent for some minutes. I wonder if he was praying Heaven to give him strength—he had to give my mother her death blow. I can never remember how he told her—in what language or fashion—but we gathered the sense of it at last; my father had left home, and had taken Miss Reinhart with him!

The blow had fallen—the worst had come. Oh, Heaven! if, sleeping or waking, I could ever forget my mother's face—if I could close my eyes without seeing its white, stony horror! The very tone of her voice was changed.

"Doctor Dalkeith!" she asked, "is this horrible thing true—true?"

"Unhappily, Lady Tayne," he replied.

"You say that my husband, Sir Roland has left me, and has gone away—with—this person?"

"I am afraid it is but too true," he replied.

"Has he ceased to love me, that he has done this?"

"My dear Lady Tayne, I know nothing but the facts—nothing else. Your servants sent for me to break it to you, for they could not bear to do it themselves."

"My servants," she said, mechanically. She still held the flowers we had gathered in her hand, the lovely sprays of mignonette! suddenly they fell to the floor, and in a strange, hoarse voice, my mother cried: "I must follow him!"

Oh, wondrous power of love! My mother, who had been crippled and helpless so long, whose feet had never taken one step; my mother suddenly stood up, her face white, her eyes filled with wild fire. She stretched out her hands—into those dead limbs of hers seemed to spring sudden life.

"I must follow them," she said, and she took what seemed to us two or three steps and then once again she fell with her face to the ground.

"I knew it would kill her," said the rector. "I told my wife so."

He rang the bell.

"Send Lady Tayne's maid here and the nurse. Send for Mrs. Dalkeith and for the doctor!"

"It has killed her, sir," said Patience, with a white face.

"I am afraid so," he replied.

They raised her and carried her to her room; they laid her down, and the rector drew me to her.

"If any voice can call her back, my dear," he said, "it will be yours; if she can hear anything it will be that. Put your arm around her neck and speak to her."

I did. But, oh, Heaven! the white face fell helplessly on mine. Oh, my beautiful young mother—as I held her there a vision came to me of her, as I had seen her, with shining eyes and flying feet.

"She is with the angels of heaven," said the rector, gently. "My poor child, come away."

"Do you mean that she is dead?" I asked—"dead?"

"Yes, she is with the angels," he replied. "Thank Heaven for it! Dear child, she could not have lived and borne this—she would have suffered a torture of anguish. Now it is all over, and she is at rest. She must have died even as she fell."

Was I dying? My face fell on hers; an exceeding bitter cry came from my lips.

"Oh, mother—mother!"

And then Heaven was merciful to me, too—a dark shadow seemed to fall over me, and I remember no more.

When I awoke I was in my own room and the sun was shining—the birds singing. Emma sat by me. Two days and two nights had passed since my mother died.

I saw her once again. She had grown more beautiful even in death; loving hands had laid white flowers on her breast and on her hands—a sweet smile was on her lips.

The rector stood there with me.

"She has been murdered," I said; "that is the right word—murdered."

60

"Yes," he replied, "murdered! But she is among the angels of heaven. Laura, loving hands have placed these flowers on your mother's silent heart; do you know, dear child, what I should like you to place in her coffin? The sweetest flower that grows."

"No; I do not know."

"The flower of divine forgiveness. I know, although you have never told me, what hot, bitter hate swells in your heart against the woman who incited your father to this sin, and even against your father himself. I do not know if we can add to the happiness of the dead; but if it be so, lay your hand on your mother's heart and say so."

After a long time I did it. I forgave them. If I meet and can talk to my mother in Heaven I will tell her why.

She was buried. No news came from my father. Tayne Hall was closed, and I went to live with my mother's cousin.

That is the story of the sin; this is the punishment:

Some years afterward Sir Roland brought his wife back to England — he married her when my mother died—-but no one would receive them. They were banished from all civilized society, and to compensate herself for that, my mother's rival mixed with the fastest and worst set in England. The end of it was that, after completely ruining him, she ran away from him and left him as he had left my mother.

His death redeemed his life. He was found dead on my mother's grave, and I loved him better in death than in life.

That is what one wicked woman can do. There is one prayer that should never leave man's lips, and it is: "Lead us not into temptation."

THE END.